The Mean Green Cleaning Machine

Written and Illustrated by
Sharon Brookhouse Suess

If it's worth doing -
It's worth doing right.
Make yourself proud!
Hugs
Sharon Suess

The Mean Green Cleaning Machine
Written and Illustrated by Sharon Brookhouse Suess

Copyright © 2014 by Sharon B. Suess
All rights reserved.

Printed by CreateSpace, an Amazon.com company

e-mail: suess@catkill.net
TheMeanGreenCleaningMachine.com
SharonSuess.com

Sharon Suess, wife, mother, grandmother, was amazed at the magnificent mess of a friend's daughter's room many years ago. Once she had grandchildren, the idea of writing a book about messy rooms bubbled to the surface. Sharon is a graphic designer, artist and writer. She has illustrated and designed numerous books for herself and others. This is the first children's book she has published. She lives in New York's Catskill Mountains with her fun-loving, supportive, incredible husband, George. (He told her to say that.)

Dedicated
to my grandchildren:
Cara
Rebecca
Neva
Ellie
&
Jack

Ellie (4 years old) drawing the
picture you see in the frames
on pages 5, 11, 13, 15, and 23.

You'd never guess
my room's such a mess.

Just open the door.
You can't see the floor!

Mommy said to clean it.
I hope she didn't mean it!

It's such a lovely mess you see.
I want to leave it; let it be.

I wish I had a cleaning machine
to clean up all this stuff.
I'd push a little button
and that would be enough.

I need to start somewhere,
there is so much to do.
And if I'm really lucky,
I'll find my other shoe.

I've been searching for it
for quite a while.
Maybe I'll find it
under the pile.

When all is orderly,
tidy and neat,

Mommy said
she'd give me a treat.

I look out my window
and start to daydream,

of my room all cleaned up
and eating ice cream.

Mommy gave me
some boxes and bags
to help me sort my stuff.

We labeled them
"Keep, Donate and Trash".
I hope they're big enough.

There are souvenirs
and glow sticks,

Baskets, books
and Halloween lips.

Paper cups
and paper clips,

Bouncing balls
and pick-up sticks.

Lots of paper,
glue and glitter.

Lots of treasure
in the litter.

Oh my, oh my,
it makes me sigh

To see the stuff
that's piled so high.

I pick up this,
I pick up that.

Where did I get
this baseball bat?

Dolls and teddy bears,
beads and string.

Cars and rings
and marbles and bling.

Big things, little things,
things stuck together.

Flip flops, pebbles,
a long peacock feather.

Paints and crayons
and a washable marker.

My mood is getting
steadily darker.

I dig deeper and deeper
under the pile.

Hey! There's my shoe!
I giggle and smile.

I fill up all the
boxes and bags.

I keep on working
though it's a drag.

Trash

Donate

Keep

Hang it from the ceiling,
tape it to the wall.

Put it on the bookcase.
Be sure it doesn't fall.

With Mommy's help
I finish my room.

We put away
the mop and broom.

I look around
and to my delight,

My room is sparkling,
clean and bright.

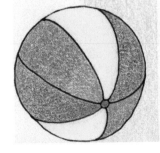

I'm proud of myself.
I actually did it.

It took a while
but I never quit it.

My Mommy is happy
and proud of me.

I should keep it clean
we both agree.

I'll clean it a little bit
now and then,

It won't ever get
that bad again.

Now that everything
Is tidy and neat,
Mommy kept her promise
And gave me a treat.

My name is Doreen.
I love the color green.
Now Mommy calls me

The
Mean Green
Cleaning Machine.

Dear Reader,

If you look closely, you can find a little mouse in each of the large illustrations. On which page is the flower, tucked in Doreen's headband, a different color?

Everything that Doreen is talking about seeing in the pile can be found in the illustration, like a search game.

I've always wanted to write and illustrate a children's book. It was more than two years in the making, and ta-dah, I finally finished it! I hope you enjoyed reading it.

> "I'm proud of myself.
> I actually did it.
> It took a while,
> but I never quit it."

Sharon Suess

Visit: TheMeanGreenCleaningMachine.com
for more information and some fun things to do.